Timothy and the Forest Folk

Timothy and the Forest Folk

Written by Marilyn Nickson
and
Illustrated by Fritz Baumgarten

7063 1154 X

Ward Lock & Co. Limited · London

Timothy lay down near a fir tree and fell fast asleep.

Timothy and the Forest Folk

Timothy lived with his mother and father in a village near a great forest. Although the family were poor and often found life hard, Timothy was a happy little fellow. His favourite pastime was to go into the forest where he loved to be with the animals and birds. Here he would feed them what crumbs he had and he loved to play music for them on his accordion.

Sometimes in the winter he would take his sledge deep into the forest, gathering firewood for his mother on the way. The chirping of the birds and the scampering noises of little animals followed him as he went. Timothy often stopped at a favourite clearing and from a sack full of nuts and cones and berries he had gathered, he would feed his many friends as they gathered around him.

It was just as well that Timothy fed the forest animals for in hard winters his was the only food they had to eat.

One winter's day Timothy was very tired from trudging through the deep snow and gathering wood. He lay down near a tall fir tree in the clearing and fell fast asleep. A gentle tug at his sleeve soon awoke him.

"Who are you?" Timothy said, with great surprise. There before him was a lively looking little chap with a snowy white beard and wearing a bright red jacket with a pointed hood.

"I'm a Firling!" said the little man in a piping voice. "I live beneath this fir tree with my other Firling friends. We have been watching while you've been resting here and have decided to help you. Come along with me!"

"But wait," said Timothy. "It's very kind of you to want to help me but I don't need any help, thank you. I must go home now. My mother will be getting worried about me."

"See how the snow has fallen and covered your tracks," said the Firling, waving his arm. "You will have to wait until springtime when the snow has gone before you can find your way home. Come along and be happy and safe with us."

Timothy was given a warm welcome by the Firlings.

The Firling skipped behind the big fir tree and Timothy followed. He opened a heavy door in the trunk of the tree and down some steps they went until they came into a large room.

"This is our home in the long, cold winter," said the Firling.

The room was full of cheerful, chattering little men all with white beards, red noses and pointed caps. They gave Timothy a warm welcome and he sat down to a lovely hot meal. His accordion puzzled them as they had never seen such a strange thing before. He was asked many questions and at last the Firling who had found him said:

"We would be very glad if you would stay with us until the winter is ended. You could help us with our work and in return we would feed and keep you. Would you like to stay?"

"Stay! Please do! Please stay!" they all cried at once. Timothy was delighted. He smiled and said:

"I'd love to stay and I promise I shall work very hard for you," replied Timothy.

Timothy worked very hard chopping logs.

"Hurrah! Hurrah!" sang all the piping voices of the Firlings around him.

Timothy kept his word and worked very hard. Every day the forest rang with the noise of his axe as he chopped wood for the Firlings. First he chopped the logs into small blocks and then he chopped the blocks into sticks. The little Firlings were surprised to see how strong he was and how hard he could work. It was a job Timothy was well used to for he often helped his mother by cutting wood for her kitchen fire.

He was never lonely living with the Firlings because, as well as them, he still had all his other friends of the forest to visit him. When he worked outdoors, they came without fail, scurrying out from the trees and bushes—the birds and the bunnies, the squirrels and the deer.

He fed them as he always had with crumbs and nuts; in fact, anything that could be spared from the little men's kitchen. And the little creatures would sit with him all day long watching him at work.

It pleased the Firlings too to see how much

Everyone had a jolly time at the Christmas Party.

All the animals and birds gathered around and ate unt

hey thought they would burst!

Timothy cared for the animals and birds for they loved them as well. They lived together very happily in their snowy forest home.

Soon it was Christmas time in the Firling village. With great excitement Timothy and the little men planned to give a grand feast for all their feathered and furry friends. They decorated their lovely fir tree with candles and put a star on the top. The tree shone with a beautiful yellow light when all the candles were lit and it made everything look cosy and warm.

Next they made a huge snowman. He was so tall that a tiny Firling had to use a stick to put his carrot nose in place! He looked like a huge white king with a crown of cones.

All the animals and birds gathered around as the Firlings fed them. They ate till they thought they would burst! Then Timothy played his accordion and taught his little friends to sing this jolly song:

Happy friends are we, singing all together,
In our forest home in the winter weather.

Happy is our song! Merrily we sing!
Through the forest tall our cheerful voices ring.
Happy friends we'll stay, joining one another,
In our work and play, merrily together."

They all had a very happy time!

One day the Firling said to Timothy, "We want to share a secret with you but you must promise never to tell anyone else, not even when you have left us to go back to your own home. Do you promise?"

"I promise," said Timothy, "cross my heart."

Then the Firlings told him of an old mine they had found under the ground when they had once been looking for a new home. They knew there was gold there but they had no tools and no idea how to begin digging it out.

"We could make our own tools," cried Timothy excitedly. "We could make picks and shovels and dig for gold. I have often watched the blacksmith in our village make tools. We could do it!"

"Good! Good!" shouted the Firlings. "Let's get started! Let's start right away!"

They built up a fire and set to work making the tools they needed. Timothy hammered the hot metal into shape when it came out of their huge fire while the Firlings made the handles of wood. After a time their picks and shovels were ready.

"Now we can start digging," said Timothy, looking very pleased with his handiwork.

There were enough tools for everyone so that they all could help with the work. They put on their little leather aprons and set off through the snow to find their mine.

They were a very merry band as they trudged along with their picks and shovels over their shoulders. Timothy decided this was a good time to teach his Firling friends another song; so this is what they sang:

We are off to work,
Down the mine we'll go!
We hope that we shall find
Gold beneath the snow.

Timothy hammered the hot metal into shape.

We'll work so very hard
Digging all day long,
And to help us on our way
We'll sing a happy song!

Their voices rang through the forest. A cheeky red squirrel decided to run along with them to see what they were up to. After all, someone had to tell all their other forest friends what all this excitement was about!

They soon found the hidden mine. The Firlings led the way down many wooden ladders. Down, down a deep dark shaft they went until they reached the tunnels below, and there, their work began.

"Listen to me," said Timothy. "Don't rush at your work or you will tire yourselves out, and do be very, very careful."

Little wooden carts were already there for them to use. They decided to ask two badger friends to do the pulling for them and they seemed very happy to help. As the carts were filled with rubble, so one of the Firlings would

Timothy and the Firlings were a very merry band.

call, "Pull away!" and off they would go to the tip.

The work was hard for the little men but they were cheerful as always. They had many different jobs to do. One was in charge of keeping the lamps lit. Some worked with picks and shovels with Timothy, helping with the digging. Another acted as the lift man turning the handle so that the lift went up and down. Some Firlings seemed to enjoy going up and down in the lift more than anything else, but even they helped when it was their turn. What a busy, bustling group they were!

One day as Timothy and the little workers were digging away at the rock, there was a cry of delight from one of the Firlings.

"We've found it! Here it is! Come quickly!"

Timothy ran over to where he was and held up his lantern. There, shining brightly, was a gleaming streak of yellow gold. It seemed to shine even more brightly than Timothy's lamp; in fact, it was just as bright as the midday sun.

They all clapped their hands and laughed with

Timothy and the Firlings worked hard in the mine.

happiness, they were so excited and pleased. Now their good friend Timothy would have gold to take back to his poor parents. They would never again have to worry about not having money enough for food or clothing, or anything else for that matter.

It did not take them long to dig out the gold. They filled the little carts with it. Next, the badgers pulled the carts to the lift and slowly and carefully, the gold was hauled up in the lift to the top of the shaft.

When they had all come out of the mine, what celebrating there was! They all jumped with delight, dancing and singing with happiness.

By this time, spring had come. Snowdrops peeped through bare patches of ground and pussy willows showed all furry on the branches. Timothy could once again find his way through the forest so it was time for him to leave the Firlings and return to his home. Soon, he would be able to tell his friends all about his new friends in the forest.

Even when saying good-bye the little Firlings

Shining brightly was a streak of yellow gold.

all smiled cheerfully. They knew that Timothy would always come back to visit his forest friends. And they would always remember the gay songs he had taught them. How could they be unhappy when they had learned to sing like him?

Timothy shook hands with each of them. As they said their good-byes, all the birds of the forest gathered, chattering noisily, as if to say good-bye in their own special way. The cheeky red squirrel who did not like to miss a thing, came back to watch everything that was happening.

Finally, with his accordion over his shoulder and his gold wrapped in a red and white handkerchief, Timothy set off through the forest. He was on his way home once more!

He soon found his path through the forest and back to his village. It was good to be there again and to see the fountain in the square and all the other things he remembered so well.

Timothy watched the pigeons playing in the water of the fountain. They reminded him sadly

All the Firlings say goodbye to Timothy.

Timothy was very pleased to see the fountain.

that he would no longer be living with the birds and animals of the forest and the Firlings.

Suddenly he remembered what he had in his red and white spotted handkerchief for his mother and father. Quickly he began to run home. It would be lovely to see his parents again, but he knew too that he would never forget his kind, happy Firling friends in the forest.

Asleep under a toadstool was Grandad Firling.

"Look! Look!" cried Monty Mouse. "There's Bertie Beetle waving to us."

"Where? Where?" said Mickey. "I can't see him."

"Up in the tree, silly," replied Monty.

"Oh, yes," said Mickey. "I wonder what he's doing up there."

"If you come on we can ask him," said Monty.

"As they walked along the forest path they suddenly came upon a little man with a long white beard, asleep under a toadstool.

"Goodness!" squeaked Mickey, "Who's that?"

"Come on, come on," shouted Bertie Beetle. "It's only Grandad Firling having his afternoon nap."

Monty, being the bravest of the two, walked ahead to greet Bertie.

"Where are we, Bertie?" said Monty. "We've walked for miles and miles and miles."

"This is Firling Town," replied Bertie. "Anyway, you must be very tired. Why not stay here . . ."

"Oh, yes, yes," cut in Mickey, whose back was aching after carrying his pack for such a long way.

"You may be tired," said Monty, "but I'm hungry."

As soon as Monty had said this Mickey also began to feel hungry.

"If you follow this path," said Bertie, "then turn right at the tall tree you will find the cake shop."

"Goody," said Mickey, who suddenly forgot his aching back and dashed along the path.

"See you later, Bertie," said Monty, and chased after Mickey.

Mickey could not believe his eyes—and certainly could not wait to have a large slice of the lovely cherry cake the Firling was slicing up.

"I'm feeling much better," said Mickey, wiping his whiskers after having eaten an enormous slice of cake.

"Let's walk round the Town," said Monty.

Mickey's mouth waters at the sight of the cherry cake.

"Then we will find somewhere to stay."

Monty and Mickey wandered round Firling Town looking at the shops and the pretty little toadstool houses.

"Everybody seems to be very busy," said Monty.

"Look! Look!" cried Mickey, pulling Monty's arm.

Under a tree were two Firlings painting the wings of a butterfly the most beautiful colours, and putting the spots on the ladybirds wings.

"Hello, young fellows," said one of the Firlings. "Would you like some red spots on your backs?"

"No! No!" said Mickey, just a little bit afraid.

"Do you paint the butterflies very often?" asked Monty.

"Only once a year for the Festival," replied the Firling.

"The Festival?" said Monty. "What's that?"

"You don't know?" replied the Firling.

"Well, we've never been to Firling Town before," said Monty.

Monty and Mickey can't believe their eyes.

"Then you came at the right time," said the Firling.

"What is it?" repeated Mickey. "What is it?"

"Have a little patience," replied the Firling, "and you will soon find out."

Poor Monty and Mickey, they were nearly crying with curiosity, but it was quite certain that the Firling was not going to tell them any more.

"Come on, Monty," said Mickey. "Let's see the other shops."

The two wandered along the street looking first in one shop and then another.

"What do you think of that," said Mickey, looking at an army of ants helping the Firlings to repair the road.

"They must be getting ready for something," replied Monty. "I'll ask them."

Stepping round the tree Monty said,

"You're very busy. Is something on?"

"Is something? Is something on?" said the Firling. "Of course something's on. The Festival Parade."

The ants help the Firlings to build the road.

"Oh," squeaked Monty.

"You're strangers here aren't you?" said the Firling.

"Yes, we only got here today," replied Monty.

"Thought as much," said the Firling. "Everybody around Firling Town has been getting ready for the Festival for days. If I were you I would go and get yourself ready."

"Can we come to the Festival?" asked Mickey.

"Of course, of course," said the Firling.

"But where can we get cleaned up?" said Monty.

"That's simple," said the Firling. "Go down to the bottom of the lane and you'll come to the shoemaker. He'll see to you."

When they reached the shoe shop the Firling said:

"Can I clean your shoes for the Festival?"

"Must they be clean?" asked Monty.

"But of course," replied the Firling. "You must look your very best."

On hearing this Mickey went to the well and washed his face and whiskers.

Mickey and Monty get ready for the Festival.

Heading the Festival Parade

vas the Froggie Jazz Band.

Just before sunset Monty and Mickey heard a band playing.

"Come on!" shouted Mickey. "It must be the Festival."

What a parade! There was the Froggie Brass Band leading a coach full to overflowing with the most delicious fruits.

"My, what a feast we'll have," cried Mickey, his mouth watering at the sight of so much food.

"You see," said the Firling painter, who stood close by. "I told you that you had come to Firling Town at the right time."

And, of course, they had.

Milly's Narrow Escape

High on the head of a daisy, waving in the breeze, Mummy Ladybird sat watching a cradle. She sang softly to her baby tucked inside. When she had finished giving her her food, she said, "Tomorrow, little Milly, I shall take off your pretty quilt and you will fly away like all other ladybirds." She tucked the blankets around Milly.

"You will soon be a grown-up ladybird and not my baby any longer," said Mummy Ladybird as she wiped a tear from her eye. "There are some things you must remember, Milly, when you go into the wide, wide world. You must know who your friends are, but—more important—you must know who your enemies are!"

But Milly felt snug in her cradle gently waving in the breeze and did not quite understand what Mummy Ladybird meant. For Milly, the wide, wide world was still far away; but she was soon to learn who were her enemies and her friends.

The next day, when the sun had risen and all the flowers were gleaming fresh with dew, Mummy Ladybird woke Milly.

"Come along, Milly! It's time to try your wings!" said Mummy.

Milly stirred very sleepily. Slowly, slowly she lifted one wing, then the other. When she was properly awake, she saw the bright blue sky and the sun shining on all the pretty flowers.

"Oh, what a lovely day! This must be the best sort of day to learn to fly," said Milly as she stretched her wings and gave a big yawn.

"First of all, Milly, open your wings wide like this," said her mother as she showed her how. "Now we shall go from the top of this daisy down to the clover stem below. Here we go!"

Off she went, sailing gracefully through the air. Milly followed quickly—too quickly! She landed suddenly with a thump far above her mother. Just as she did, a beautiful creature with huge wings flew up from a cluster of buttercups.

"Oooh!" said Milly to her mother, "What a

Mummy Ladybird sat watching Milly in her cradle.

lovely thing! Whatever is it?"

"That," replied Mummy Ladybird, "is a butterfly."

"Not just any old butterfly," her mother went on. "He is the Red Admiral and is known throughout the world as one of the loveliest of us all."

The Red Admiral flew away with a graceful sweep of its beautifully coloured wings.

"He is one of our friends, but let me tell you, Milly," her mother warned, "that not everyone in the world is our friend."

Then her mother told her about big Black Spiney, the caterpillar, and of his prison where he locks up all the insects he can catch. He keeps them to fatten them up and then sells them to the birds for food.

"You must never go near the roots of the old oak tree, Milly," said her mother, "for that is where Black Spiney's prison is!"

With that, she left Milly, who then soared off into the wide, wide world on her own.

Milly next found herself on a stem beside

A beautiful butterfly with huge wings flew by.

someone who looked just like a ladybird except that he had red spots on a black back.

"Good-day," he said politely, as he tipped his tiny hat to Milly.

"Good-day," replied Milly. "Are we cousins?"

"Yes, of course we are!" was the reply. "I am Tony, your first cousin. Can't you tell from the colours on my back?"

Milly squinted hard and tried to see him as orange and black instead of black and orange.

"I say," said Tony, "I saw a terrible sight just a few minutes ago. A family of robins—seven babies! And their mother and father were feeding them as fast as they could!"

"Is that bad?" asked Milly.

"Bad?" said Tony. "It's disastrous, that's what it is! Think of all the food they'll want when they grow up. It makes me shudder! I'm off to a safer place. Good-bye, cousin!"

With these words. Tony tipped his hat once more and off he flew.

Milly left her stem and slowly floated in the air, looking all about her. Suddenly she saw a

Milly found herself sitting on a stem with her cousin.

frightening sight. There, in front of her, were two birds and in a nest-box no less than seven large, gaping, hungry mouths! Milly shuddered with fear, lost her balance, and fell straight down to the ground.

Luckily for Milly she landed on a patch of soft moss.

"My, my," said Georgie Grasshopper. "You should watch what you are doing."

"Who are you?" asked Milly, knowing that the little creature who was speaking to her meant no harm to her.

"I'm Georgie Grasshopper and this is my home," he replied.

"Please forgive me, but I was so frightened," said Milly.

"Yes, you must be careful of those birds," answered Georgie. "They'll gobble you up in no time at all."

"I'll be very careful," said Milly.

"If I were you," continued Georgie, "I would keep to the low bushes."

Milly thanked Georgie Grasshopper and flew

There were no less than seven hungry mouths.

off. She had not gone very far when she came upon a little pond. Milly was fascinated as she had never seen a pond before. Fish were darting about in the water and ducks were swimming about quacking to each other.

"I would fly away from here," said a voice.

Milly turned, only to find her cousin, Tony, sat next to her.

"Tony!" exclaimed Milly. "I was only looking."

"It's looking that's dangerous," said Tony. "You may get giddy and fall, and if the ducks don't eat you up the fish will."

"My goodness," said Milly. "Is anywhere safe?"

"Yes, if you're careful," replied Tony.

Together Milly and Tony flew away from the pond. For a long time they played in and out of the low bushes.

"Tony," said Milly, "I'm going to have a rest."

"Okay, I'll see you later," said Tony. "But remember to keep out of the way of horrible old Black Spiney."

There in front of Milly was dreaded Black Spiney.

"I will," said Milly, and flew up into a nearby tree.

Poor Milly, she was much more tired than she thought. She had only intended to have a rest, but it was not long before she was fast asleep. She had not been asleep long when a sharp gust of wind blew her off her perch.

Caught unawares Milly fell to the ground only to land on her back with her little legs in the air and her wings spread out. As she struggled to turn herself over, Milly spotted a great hole in the ground. Crawling out from it came a huge, black ugly caterpillar. It was the dreaded Black Spiney!

Black Spiney was worse than anything Milly had ever imagined. He had a horrible face—beady eyes and a nasty looking moustache. He had so many spines on his back, you couldn't count them.

"Ah, ha! Oh, Ho!" he cried in a gritty voice. "What have I here? You look good enough to eat!"

"Oh, dear!" cried Milly. "I'm just learning to

fly. It's my first day in the wide, wide world. Please let me go!"

"What? Let you go?" laughed Black Spiney. "You are just what I am looking for. A little bit of fattening up and you will fetch a pretty price."

"No, no. Please don't lock me up," cried Milly. But Black Spiney laughed again and frightened poor Milly even more. He crawled even closer to her.

"You come along with me now," said the gritty voice. "You are my prisoner!"

Milly was led away to the bottom of the old oak tree. There, in the roots, was the prison. Each cell had a strong barred door fastened with a big padlock. Once inside, it looked as though it would be impossible ever to get out.

Black Spiney led little Milly to one of the cells. He opened the door and pushed her inside. There was a horrible "clank" as he locked the padlock. Off went Black Spiney, chuckling to himself.

Poor little Milly. How she cried and cried. What a noise she made!

"I should have done what cousin George did," she moaned, "and gone to a safer place. I should have taken notice of what mother said!"

Milly felt very sorry for herself indeed.

Just then, there was a swishing sound in the air. Milly looked through the bars of the cell door and there was a handsome butterfly landing gently in front of Milly's prison. He had quite different markings from the Red Admiral who was the only butterfly Milly had seen, but, thought Milly, he *must* be a friend.

"I will get help," whispered the butterfly. "You must be brave. I will fetch Larry. He will know how to get you out!"—and off he flew.

Milly stopped crying and began to feel a little less sad.

"Who is Larry?" she wondered to herself. Whoever he was, she hoped the butterfly was right and that he would get her out of this dark, dank prison.

At that moment, the friendly butterfly had found Larry somewhere else in the wood. Larry

The butterfly said he would go and find Larry.

was another ladybird, very handsome and very kind. When he heard of Milly's sad plight, he knew he must free her before it was too late.

He, too, had once been Black Spiney's prisoner but he had been lucky enough to escape. Larry knew that at about noon every day, Black Spiney went digging for grubs under rocks. If he could get to the prison just about that time, he might be able to free Milly.

Larry went off to find his two beetle friends.

"You watch on this side of the rocks, Bulgy," he said to one, "and you on the other side, Batty. If Black Spiney leaves the rocks, you must warn me. I shall be at the prison trying to free poor Milly."

Off he soared through the air, leaving Bulgy and Batty to keep watch on dreaded Black Spiney as he dug under the rocks.

"Hallo, Milly," said Larry when he reached the prison. "I've come to rescue you."

"Are you Larry?" she cried. "Oh, I am pleased to see you! Please, please get me out!"

"Don't be afraid, Milly. My friends Bulgy and

Black Spiney went digging for grubs under some rocks.

Batty are keeping watch over Black Spiney while I try to free you. Quickly, can you tell me where he has hidden the key?"

"Under the stone by the last cell. Oh please hurry!" cried Milly.

Larry found the key, quick as a wink. He unlocked Milly's cell first and then all the others. Soon Black Spiney had no prisoners left! Everyone thanked Larry for being so brave and kind, and flew away as fast as they could. No one wanted to be there when their horrible enemy returned!

Larry and Milly flew away together. By the evening they were sitting together on a berry bush.

Now they had both grown very fond of each other and decided to marry, so together they planned a huge wedding to which they would invite all their friends.

What a wedding it was! Milly had eight ladybirds to carry her beautiful white lace train, and Larry carried a very smart top hat.

The sun shone bright and the bluebells and

Milly and Larry rest on a berry bush.

buttercups and daisies looked down on all the friends who had come from far and near.

There were ants and bees, beetles and grasshoppers. Even slow Sam Snail managed to get there on time! Mr. Mole, very handsome in a white lace collar, read the wedding service. He stumbled a little over some of the words for, even with his glasses, he could not see too well. There was music from the humming bees who danced about in the flowers while the wedding took place.

A great feast was held afterwards. Black Spiney and all the horrors of the prison were soon forgotten. Milly and Larry were very happy and, together with their friends, they sang and danced all day long.

"Tomorrow Milly, we shall have to look for a snug little home," said Larry. "Winter must not catch us with nowhere to live."

"I know just the place!" said the faithful friendly butterfly. "I will show you first thing in the morning."

Sure enough, the first thing next morning the

Eight ladybirds carried Milly's beautiful lace train.

Milly and Larry in their snug little house.

butterfly came for Milly and Larry. Together they flew, as the butterfly guided them to the foot of a fir tree.

"Here we are!" he said to the two ladybirds. "Look at this lovely little hollow under the roots. You will be very cosy here."

Milly was very excited.

"It's lovely! It's just what we want, isn't it Larry?" Please may we stay?" she asked.

And they did. By the time the first snow had fallen, they had furnished their little home and were very snug indeed with a warm fire and lots to eat.

With this happy beginning, Milly and Larry lived happily ever after.

Impreso en los talleres de EDITORIAL FHER, S. A.
BILBAO (España)

PRINTED IN SPAIN